INVISIBLE ENCOUNTER

Published under licence by Brown Dog Books and
The Self-Publishing Partnership Ltd, 10b Greenway Farm, Bath Rd,
Wick, nr. Bath BS30 5RL

www.selfpublishingpartnership.co.uk

ISBN printed book: 978-1-83952-610-7
ISBN e-book: 978-1-83952-611-4

Cover design by Andrew Prescott
Internal design by Andrew Easton

Printed and bound in the UK

This book is printed on FSC® certified paper

INVISIBLE ENCOUNTER

COLIN GIBBINS

BROWN
DOG
BOOKS

INVISIBLE ENCOUNTER

COLIN GIBBINS

Mike Walton was born in 1965 in the northeast of England. He was the only child of Robert and Mary. Robert had served in the army for twenty years but left to look after Mary, who was in ill health. He was a tall burly man with thick dark hair and a happy laid-back demeanour and had served in the Commandos for ten of those years and he was decorated for bravery while in action. They lived in small cottage on a large country estate where he worked as a gamekeeper responsible for the livestock, a large forest and a pheasant farm.

As a young boy Mike not only looked like his father with his thick dark hair and stocky build but shared his father's love of the great outdoors, spending his time exploring the beautiful estate with its lush green pastures ablaze with brightly scented flowers and shrubs with a sparkling silver river meandering through the middle. This serene atmosphere blending with the song of abundant bird life created a truly idyllic World for him. But his greatest love was tending the livestock and walking through the forest learning about nature. And as the sun filtered through the forest canopy creating a magical yet eerie atmosphere his imagination ran wild.

Dressed in his army uniform and armed with his toy gun he moved stealthily through the undergrowth tracking imaginary enemies.

Sadly his mother died when he was ten and he became closer to his father, spending all his spare time working on the estate. Over the following years Robert showed Mike everything there was to know about living off the land, hunting, shooting and survival training he himself had learned while in the Commandos. At the age of fifteen Mike was fully trained in the art of survival, in the peak of fitness and very self-confident.

On leaving school Mike enrolled as an army cadet based in Catterick camp. Robert drove him there and walked with him up to the barrier at the camp entrance. He wrapped his arms around his son. 'Your mother would have been so proud to see you in your uniform,' he said fighting back the tears. 'She always knew you would follow in my footsteps, please stay safe and keep in contact, updating me on your progress.' Mike too was struggling to keep his emotions under control, this would be the first time he would be parted from his beloved father. 'You needn't worry. I will make you proud of me, all the time and effort you have spent training me will be so important and I'm sure will keep me safe.'

With one last warm embrace Mike took a long deep breath, showed his pass at the gatehouse, turned waved at his father before throwing back his shoulders and marched up the yard and into the main office. He soon settled in and became popular in the camp with his officers and fellow cadets through his happy confident nature and although so experienced he remained modest and mild mannered. So it was no surprise that at the end of his two year training he ended up top cadet.

At the age of eighteen he was in peak condition and with all the physical and strenuous training his body was fully developed, looking more like his tall burly built father. He was overjoyed when he received his first posting to Northern Ireland, but this was a dangerous place to be and when he arrived he quickly discovered this was going to be so different from his experience in the Cadet Camp. The environment was so different in the Cadet Camp, they were all around the same age so it was obvious he would stand out with his father's training, but these new comrades were in the main hardened soldiers, rough tough men, most of whom had served in various conflicts.

They enjoyed a laugh and particularly winding up new recruits but after several training sessions most of them were impressed by this new boy's qualities and his calm approach to difficult situations. At first he was on guard duty at the base, which wasn't his idea of soldiering, and he pestered the officers to give him more tasking roles. Finally after two months he joined patrols around the towns and checkpoints and again showed bravery and intuition.

After six months all the new recruits were accessed and reviewed by the Colonel to determine whether they were suitable to be deployed in their operations. Mike was little nervous as he made his way along the corridor to the Colonel's office, he stopped at the door straightened his tie and uniform took a deep breath before knocking. The door opened and one of the guards ushered him into the room. Mike looked so tense as he stood before Colonel James seated at his desk with an officer sitting either side of him.

The Colonel looked up. 'At ease, Mike, you're not being court marshalled, just a short appraisal of your time here, your qualities and weaknesses if any. I have to say you are one of the best recruits we have had in a long time, but I see why looking through your records. I see your father was a commando and you were brought up on a country estate, so I'm assuming that is where your skills were formed'.

Mike again took a deep breath. 'Yes sir, I spent all my childhood following my father around the estate and sleeping and foraging in the forest.' A warm smile spread across the Colonel's face. 'Yes, I can see that would be the perfect introduction to army life, so we have decided to let you join our team of troops who are responsible for stakeouts of IRA arms dumps and the ambush of suspected IRA operations.' He paused a moment. 'I don't have to tell you these are dangerous operations, but you are well trained and will be fully briefed before going out on surveillance.' The Colonel stood up shook Mikes hand, Mike stepped back, saluted before marching out of the room with a huge relieved and contented smile on his face.

Mike as usual was impatient as he waited for his first operation, becoming more and more frustrated as the days passed by. Finally he was called to briefing room to join his team. John Williams a stocky rugged happy go lucky guy, the joker in the team. Tim Watson a communications expert, and Joe Lawson an army sniper. Intelligence had been received that the IRA was planning an attack on a prison on the outskirts of Ulster where six of their important fighters were being held. After the briefing they immediately made their way in an unmarked van with a motorbike rider following behind and they travelled over to the rear of a terraced house which overlooked the prison.

After unloading all their equipment, water, food, weapons, ammunition, communication and surveillance devices, the motorbike was left with them and the rider joined the van driver and they sped off. Mike parked the motorbike in the back yard while the rest of the team carried the equipment up the stairs, making sure they made no noise. After sorting out all the equipment they climbed into the attic and quietly slipped out one of the roof slates and took it in turns to keep watch over the jail using their night vision goggles.

On the third night it was Mikes' watch. He was becoming impatient, Tim and Joe were asleep in the corner while John sat beside Mike propped up against the wall. Mike glanced over to John. 'Do you think they will attack tonight?' John shrugged his shoulders. 'You ask that they every time you are on watch, just relax. Could be tonight could be next week.' Mike sighed out. 'I just hope it's on my watch.' John glanced up at Mike shook his head as he noticed an excited smile on his face 'this is the real thing. Not cowboys and Indians, it will happen when it happens, just try and relax,' he said before closing his eyes and making himself comfortable.

Some time later John was in a deep sleep when Mike shook him awake. 'John a black car passed the prison a few minutes ago slowing down as it did, it returned a few minutes later and again crawled past.' Mike watched as the car turned at the top of the road and headed back. 'It's turned again.' John detached himself from the wall. 'What's happening now?' Mike looked intently through the goggles. 'Three men have got out. You had better wake Tim and Joe.' John was already crawling over to the two soldiers and shook them awake. They reacted automatically. Joe grabbed his rifle while Tim set up radio contact with HQ, John joined Mike and put on his night vision goggles. Mike moved away as John took over. He watched one of the three men inspect the tyres of the black car while the other two lit up cigarettes, casually glancing towards the prison. 'All three men took one last look before quietly climbing back into the car,' John whispered.

Mike jumped up grabbed a pistol, two hand grenades and a radio before rushing over to the hatch. 'I'll keep in contact,' he said as he climbed down to the landing and scuttled down the stairs, leaving the other three taken aback by Mikes' instant reaction giving them no time to argue or discuss the next move. Mike opened the back gate and rode the motorbike out and was soon heading in the direction of the black car.

They headed out of the city for about two miles then turned off up a dirt track road towards what seemed to be a farm. Mike road past the road and continued further up the main road, about a half a mile further on there was another turn off heading in the same direction as the first dirt track.

He hid the bike and headed up the track on foot. He could see a small hut up ahead. Using a small telescope he could see a guard through the window. As Mike crept up to the hut he could see the guard sitting reading, and that his rifle was propped up against the table. Mike crept around the front and kicked the door clown and ran inside. He overpowered the guard and bound and gagged him. He took the rifle and the ammunition that was on the table before heading up the track. There was gate at the top and Mike, using his telescope, could see the buildings some half a mile further on. As he got closer he could make out a house and a few barns and byres. There was a large furniture van outside one of the barns. Using his telescope he could see there were ten men loading the van with explosives. The black car and another three vehicles parked alongside the van.

Mike contacted Tim back at the observation house and told him to radio HQ. He would wait till the troops arrived and keep him updated of any further development. There was a barn opposite the house as Mike crept inside. He used his night vision goggles as he searched the building; it was empty and the loft made an excellent observation point. He could see that they were loading explosives, the other outbuilding looked empty but he could see a light on in the house. As he focused on the window he could see someone bound and gagged in a chair. He waited a while and contacted Tim, who told him the troops would be there in half an hour.

Mike assumed the man in the window was the farmer. If so, what would happen to him when the troops arrived? Maybe the terrorists would use him as a hostage or shoot him, so Mike decided to investigate. He crept around the back of the house, looking through the window he could see one guard sitting on a chair with his rifle beside him. The man Mike had seen gagged and bound was there with what looked like his family, a women and two children also gagged and bound.

Mike was sure they would be used as hostages when the troops arrived and could ruin the mission and might even be harmed. He picked up a metal bar that was lying against the house; he knew he would only get one blow to silence the guard otherwise they were all dead. He slowly opened the back door and crept in, the door into the room they were in was open slightly and the guard had his back to Mike. As he crept in the guard turned towards Mike and in a split second the bar was crashing down. The guard was knocked off his chair and he lay still. Once he was bound and gagged he freed the captives and asked if they had any transport. The man said he was a farmer and they were his family and they had a Land Rover parked at the rear in one of the barns. Mike told him to take his family to the Land Rover and be prepared to start the engine and head down the track once he heard an explosion. He told him the troops would be there shortly so he must wait for them to arrive and tell them the layout and details of the terrorists.

Mike had two rifles now and a few grenades, he escorted the family out of the back door and to the Land Rover before turning back around to the hay barn. He left the rifles inside and went back outside and crept closer to the van and the terrorists. He threw two grenades towards the van before he sprinted back to the hay barn. There was a huge explosion as he carried the rifles up to the loft. When the smoke cleared he could see the van was destroyed and there were at least four bodies on the ground. One of the other vehicles had been damaged, using his rifle he blasted the tyres of the other vehicles to prevent them escaping. In the distance he could see the Land Rover heading down the track. Mike smiled, they were safe. Then he saw a head looking out of the barn, Mike fired and the head disappeared, he would keep them pinned down until the troops arrived.

Shortly after the troopers came up the dirt track, some forty men, and circled the barn. The three terrorists still alive threw out their weapons and surrendered. Mike told the troopers where the other two terrorists he had tied up could be found and got a lift back down to where he had left his bike. The farmer was waiting with his family. As Mike got out of the truck the farmer and his wife wrapped their arms around him, no words were needed.

Mike joined his team back at the observation house and they made their way back to HQ, he knew he would be in trouble for not following orders. The Colonel was waiting for them but told Mike to have a shower and a sleep; he would speak with him the next morning.

The following day Mike was escorted to the interview room. The Colonel was seated at the table with two officers and the Staff Sergeant. He was asked to go through the events of the previous day from when he left the observation house and give details and reason for his actions. They then asked him several questions before he was told to wait outside and he would be recalled in due course. After what seemed an eternity he was told to return and remain standing while the Colonel spoke. He said although the outcome had been a success Mike had disobeyed orders and he had not only put the mission in jeopardy but he had endangered both his own life and the lives of the farmer and his family. These Maverick tactics could not be tolerated by the regular army and were more suited to the Special Forces. The SAS needed men who could make instant decisions and act on them in life or death situations and he was asked whether he had ever considered the Special Forces.

The Colonel said that Mike had been their star student and that his attitude, dedication and character were first class, and if he wished he would recommend him to the Special Forces. So, at the age of twenty, Mike travelled down to Stirling Lines in Hereford to start the selection course to become a member of the 22nd Special Air Service Regiment.

When he arrived there were about seventy-five volunteers from different sections of the army and all parts of the country. They were told to assemble in the mess room and the commander-in-chief, Lieutenant Colonel James Brown, would speak to them. He welcomed them to camp and said that the next few weeks would be the hardest and longest of their lives. This would sort out the right men with the qualities required by regiment. He said most of them would either quit or be sent home before the course had ended. The regiment needed soldiers of the highest calibre, men who under terrible conditions could act, think and push themselves to the limit and beyond. They had to be tough not only physically but mentally, and be able to come up with solutions for situations quickly in life-threatening conditions. He told them that exercises started the following morning at 4 AM and that they should have an early night. After he left they talked among themselves and Mike met a young American, Steve Kennedy who had just been accepted into the American Special Force Delta Force. He had been sent to Hereford to learn the SAS techniques to improve his fitness, by Delta Force's commander-in-chief Steve Jackson. Mike and Steve hit it off immediately, they had so much in common, even Steve's father had served in the Commandos but he had been killed in Vietnam.

Next day they were awakened at 3.30 AM. and out on the parade ground they met Sergeant Jim Baxter, a big rough-looking Scot. They split into groups of five and were given a map, compass, rifle and a Bergan (pack), the sergeant then marked several rendezvous points on the map. There was a time limit between the RV points but they were still not told of the times as they must march as fast as they can or jog. The marches started over the Black Mountains and each day the distance increased, as did the weight of the Bergans. As the weeks go by they march alone and the marches extend to South Wales and the harsh terrain of the Brecon Beacons. As they reach each RV they are given a task to perform again with a time limit, maybe a war like situation and they have to come up with a solution and act on their decision.

They return to camp at eleven PM wet and exhausted, all they want to do is sleep and be ready for the following day's exercise. After the third week there was only twenty-five left from the original seventy-five, some have left others sent home. Mike and Steve become good friends the more they talked the more they realised how much they had in common and that the most important thing in their lives was the Army. Steve showed him pictures of his family and his girlfriend Louise, but Mike was glued to the pictures of Steve's sister, Holly. She was the most beautiful girl he had ever seen. She had bright blue eyes and long golden hair, she was eighteen years old and a university student, studying law. Mike turned to Steve.

'Has she got a boyfriend?'

Steve smiled. 'Not anyone serious but at the end of this course I'm going home for two weeks and you are welcome to come with me and meet Holly.'

The following morning Sergeant Baxter was waiting for them on the parade ground and informed them they had to now face the test week, a forty mile march known as the 'long drag' which has to be completed in twenty hours over mountains and rough terrain. They set off one by one alone with their heavy Bergans, exhausted by the previous three weeks they pushed on through the pain barrier, with only the super fit finishing the course.

They gathered on the parade ground in front of Lieutenant Colonel James Brown. Only fifteen had passed, the Colonel glanced over the tired faces. 'Congratulations on your effort to complete the four weeks of marches. I am pleased to see our young American friend Steve Kennedy is lasting the course.

There is, however, a long way to go before being accepted into the regiment. You will have one week's leave before returning to undergo four months of continuation training.' He made his way over to the volunteers to shake their hands and have a word with each of them, Sergeant Baxter walked closely behind.

The Colonel smiled as he shook Mike's hand. 'Congratulations, Mike, your father must be a proud man today.' He turned and raised his hand as he left them chatting amongst themselves.

Mike put his hand on Steve's shoulder. 'We have a week's leave. Would you like to come up to Durham with me and meet my father?'

Steve smiled and nodded. 'Yes it would be an honour to meet him.'

Mike and Steve travelled by train up to Durham and Robert was there to meet them. He fought back his tears as he wrapped his arms around his son. He turned to Steve and shook his hand, Robert was so proud he could see that Mike had turned into a fine young man and that he had formed a close relationship with Steve. The three of them enjoyed the week together, camping, shooting and just walking through the forest laughing, chatting and swapping past experiences. Steve enjoyed Roberts company and he reminded him of his own father they shared the same love of their country and their army life.

After they said their goodbyes they travelled back down to Hereford to join their comrades to go through the continuation training. Steve was told the commander of Delta Force had requested him to stay and go through the continuation training. This four-month training concentrated on the skills needed to become an SAS trooper: demolitions, weapons training, first aid, signalling and methods of reconnaissance and survival. They went through all of these basic operating procedures, learning Morse code, being able to transmit and receive map reading and field medicine.

The first three weeks they went on survival training on Exmoor, learning how to live off the land in hostile conditions laying traps, searching for food, berries and plants, building shelter from whatever was available and seeking out water. Then for three days they went on evasion exercise, living off the land while being hunted down by army infantry. The next exercise was interrogation. They were tested as they would be if captured by the enemy using physical and psychological methods to break their spirit and if they cracked they were rejected.

The final test saw them split into four-man units and sent to the Far East for jungle training, and if one of the men in the unit failed the whole unit had failed. Once this was successfully completed, plus a basic parachute course, they were accepted into the Regiment. So Mike was one of only twelve out of the original seventy-five to become a trooper in the 22nd SAS Regiment. They were told they had two weeks' leave and then to report back.

Steve had completed the course and would go home on leave for two weeks and then rejoin Delta Force. Again he asked Mike to come with him and meet his family, Mike didn't need to be asked twice. He had never been to America and was very excited as they boarded the plane and could not wait to meet Holly. After landing at LA Airport, Steve's mother was there to greet them and drive them to their home in San Fernando Valley City.

Their home was a smallholding outside the city and the house was a timber ranch-style building with beautiful views. They went inside and the table was set for a meal. Steve's mother Jane said they would have a drink and snack then have a meal when Holly got back from college.

Some two hours later as they sat chatting the door opened and Holly walked in. Steve introduced her to Mike. He stood up and stuttered a few words. They all laughed, she was even more beautiful that the picture Steve had shown him. As she shook his hand his heart was pounding. He felt a little more comfortable as they enjoyed their meal and chatted. It was very difficult to take his eyes off her.

After the meal Steve told Holly to show Mike around

the smallholding while he talked to his mother to catch up on the local gossip. They came out of the house and walked through the garden. Holly asked Mike about his family and his interests outside of the army. The more they talked they realised how much they had in common. Mike felt so relaxed with her as though they had known each other for years.

Over the next two weeks Mike spent his days with Steve looking around the area and meeting Steve's friends and at night after dinner he spent time with Holly. They just walked and talked. Mike's feelings were getting stronger by the day but he knew Holly was very young and she lived so far away. Steve spent his time with his girlfriend Louise and some nights the four of them would go out together. On the last night they all went to a dance at Holly's college and Mike and Holly danced all night. He was falling in love with this wonderful girl. At the end of the night she gave him a kiss and promised to keep in touch and write each week.

Next day they said their farewells and Mike said he would keep in touch and visit again. Steve drove him to the airport and waved him off. On the flight back home Mike went over the past two weeks and his feelings for Holly and what lay ahead. His future was with the SAS and if in time the relationship with Holly blossomed that would be fantastic.

When he got back to Hereford he was told to go and see the Colonel; he told Mike his father had been killed in a shooting accident on his estate. Mike went back home for the funeral and as he left the estate he glanced back and knew this would be the last time he would see the old place. Back at HQ he joined the rest of his troop and they were told they would be flying out to Iraq the next day and would be briefed on arrival. That night the colonel, James Brown, came to see Mike. He told Mike his father would be proud of him and that if he needed to talk he was always there. James took a shine to Mike the first time they met and as the selection course progressed he could see that Mike was a special young man, a leader and a great asset to the regiment.

Next day the full squadron flew out to the United Arab Emirates to start desert training. Their base camp was in Saudi Arabia. Once they had settled in they were briefed on the situation. This was August 1990 and 100,000 Iraqi troops had crossed their border into Kuwait. They would have probably four or five months to train prior to war breaking out, enough time to acclimatise to the environment and conditions. They soon found out that things had been rushed and there was a shortage of weapons, equipment, maps of the country and general intelligence information. Most of the older troopers moaned a little but in true SAS tradition just got on with the job using, what little they had and improvising where needed. They were told that the war would be fought mainly in the air and that the US Special Force and Marines would carry out the reconnaissance that they would normally be engaged in. This would leave them with a free role to hit targets of opportunity, to cross the border in their given zones and to deal with situations that they would encounter.

For the following few weeks the squadron went through desert training to cope with the heat and terrain with limited resources. The officers would assess the new troopers. Mike was one of the five attached to the squadron and the strengths and weakness of each one soon became apparent. This would allow the officers to split the squadron into groups, with each group needing troopers with skills in weapons, demolition, communication and first aid, with some having a natural talent for mountaineering, martial arts and reconnaissance. Mike was selected for reconnaissance because of his survival skills and his ability to assess situations and act under pressure, as he had done in Northern Ireland, and the training he had been given by his father. So he was very proud not only for himself but to the memory of his father when he was selected as one of a two-man foot patrol carrying out reconnaissance for the main troop.

At the beginning of January 1991 war broke out and the SAS squadrons were moved to their operating base the same night. Early next morning they were on the move. Each group had its own zone to work in and had to select the best place to make their crossing into Iraq. Mike and a big Scottish trooper, Andy O'Neal, were to act as a forward patrol for their squadron. That night the two searched along the border looking for a safe crossing point armed with American M16 rifles with attached grenade launchers, hand grenades and night vision goggles.

They crossed over into central Iraq, after making sure the area was safe and clearly they contacted the main troop who followed and joined up. They pushed on during the night and before dawn found a place to hole up during the night. Taking turns on watch the rest of the troop slept under their camouflage nets ready for the night-search for targets.

Mike was on watch and his mind turned to Holly and Steve. Maybe he would bump into Steve as Delta Force was working in Iraq. Maybe they would team up on operations jointly carried out by the two special forces. This was the reason he had joined the army to be in this situation fighting for his country in different parts of the world. The next two days were very much the same, pushing further into Iraq territory during the night and hiding during the day.

Iraq had an advanced communications network; high relay towers boosted signals passed through fibre optic cables which were buried underground. American aircraft had bombed a communication complex in the area Mike's squadron were operating in so he and Andy would carry out the close target recons to see what damage had been done. Using their night vision goggles they made their way to the main gate of the complex. There was a guard but they were able to slip past into the compound. They could see the damage caused by the aircraft but the main tower was still standing and in operation. The Iraqis had machine guns sited at the four corners of the compound and the troops looked like they were expecting the aircraft to return as they did not see Mike and Andy slip back out of the gates.

After briefing the main troop the plan was that a ten-man team would enter the compound in twos, Mike and Andy would go first. Once inside they would regroup under the tower then while the two demolition experts set the explosives around the tower, the other eight would split into four teams, they would be responsible for taking out the four machine gun positions while outside the main troop set up their weapons ready to cover the retreating troops once the job was complete. Once the explosives were set the two demolition troopers worked their way back to the main gate and waited to detonate. Then on a signal the other troopers threw hand grenades into the four machine gun positions and then joined the other two, who detonated the explosives. The ten troopers made their way back through the gate while the main troop fired mortar and machine guns to cover the retreat. They could see the tower was down and the complex was ablaze and completely out of action.

Over the next three weeks Mike's squadron destroyed three mobile scud launchers and several watchtowers and were able to ambush several convoys of equipment. At the end of the campaign Mike met up with Steve. Delta Force had been engaged in blowing up mobile scud launchers and he too had a successful mission. They were both due for leave and again Mike went with Steve back to America to spend it with his family.

The next ten years saw Mike engaged in missions all over the world. From time to time he would meet up with Steve and they both became top men in their regiments. They were both decorated for their bravery while in action and were respected by their officers and fellow troopers. Any leave they had would be spent with Steve's family, Holly was now a Lawyer with her own practice and was still single – a real career girl.

Steve was the leader of his squadron in Delta Force and his men felt he was their talisman, with success after success in missions all over the world.

Meanwhile Mike was thought to be the SAS regiment's best reconnaissance man, earning the name 'Scot'. he would go behind enemy lines to gather information and intelligence needed for the success of that mission. This was the main reason the SAS had been as successful; secrecy was the most important tool in war, hence the name 'Ghost Force'.

Then in 2003 they were back in the Gulf as war with Iraq loomed again. Three weeks into the invasion Mike and Steve's squadrons were to work together to attack one of the Iraqi Army Divisions. Mike went ahead on recon with a member of Delta Force, he would follow Mike but stay some hundred yards behind. As Mike got near to the camp he was on his hands and knees. As he crawled nearer he touched a land mine and it exploded. When the other trooper reached Mike he could see his arm had been blown off just below the elbow, he tried to stop the bleeding and contacted their main troop. By this time the Iraqi soldiers had opened fire and had them pinned down.

Steve led the rescue team and they managed to get Mike back to base. Next day he was flown back to England. It took a few weeks for the limb to heal enough to start trying to be fitted with a false limb. He had been transferred to the Queen Mary's Hospital in Roehampton, one of the world's leading workshops for state-of-the-art prosthetic limbs. Usually the physiotherapists have to build up the muscles to the back and shoulders to be able to carry and work the limb. Mike would not need this as he was in peak condition with all his training. The prosthetics made a cast of the limb, the first of many, each one fit better and finally it was a perfect fit.

Mike was a willing patient and worked so hard. The fact he was in such good physical condition meant the damaged limb had plenty of tissue and residual muscle, which gives off a small electrical discharge when the muscle is tensed up. This electrical discharge opens the hand and when the muscle relaxes the hand closes. After two weeks Mike had the hand working really well, able to pick up things and put them back down. But even the most high tech limbs in the world would be no substitute for a real limb and Mike knew his life would never be the same again.

Three weeks after going into hospital he returned to HQ and was pleased to be back with the regiment and his fellow troopers. Next day he had a meeting with Colonel James Brown to discuss his future. Was he to be discharged? Mike could not bear to consider life outside the army. The Colonel had always liked Mike and knew what the army meant to him so he told Mike he could stay, maybe at first a desk job, and then in time become involved with the training of the new cadets. This would enable him to pass on the experience and knowledge he had gained over the years to the next generation of troopers.

Mike asked for time to think things over and so he packed some equipment and made off to Exmoor. This was where he had done his training. It was so isolated and he would be able to think things over without being disturbed. He soon realised that his false arm had changed things. Simple tasks were much more difficult and active duty would be impossible. That night he lay in his tent looking up at the stars; he felt at peace with himself for the first time since his accident.

Next morning after breakfast he went walking on the moors, he lost track of time and realised it was turning dusk. He made his way back to camp and as he got close he saw a bright light move over the top of him and drop down behind some trees a few hundred yards past his tent. He went to investigate and in the clearing beyond the trees was a single craft with lights flashing.

As a young boy and into his adult life Mike had been interested in the stars and extra-terrestrial encounters and abductions. This craft was very much as he had imagined: disc shaped, dull aluminium metallic in colour, the shape was like two shallow dishes welded together. There was no visible seam. On top of the dish was a raised dome with part holes in the dome and tower dish. The craft was approximately two hundred feet in diameter and thirty feet deep. The dome was about five feet above the top dish and about fifty feet in diameter. There were lights around the centre and on the top and bottom and were pulsating.

On landing the craft had three extendable legs with large pads on their base. As the craft came to land it hovered above the ground and the legs extended down to solid ground, keeping the craft level and about three feet off the ground. A hatch at the lower part of the dish dropped down to form a ramp to gain access. As Mike watched it drop he thought about what he had read about encounters. All the recorded encounters and abductions had resulted in the aliens taking the abductees onto the craft and after carrying out various tasks they are then released. So as the ramp touched the ground and four aliens came down and over towards him Mike did not feel this was life threatening. He felt he had been in worse situations. One thing he remembered was that fear had always made the situation worse. The aliens had then hypnotised the abductees and his SAS training in mind over matter was about to be tested.

As they got nearer he could see they had tight-fitting shiny silver uniforms with a large belt around the waist and boots and they had some writing or markings on their chests. They stood about four feet tall, with large oval heads and large dark eyes at an angle which wrapped around the side of their face. Their face had no projections with only slots for nose, mouth and ears. Their skin was very pale with a greyish cast and they had no hair. Their legs were very short with longer arms in comparison with four long fingers on their hands.

They stopped in front of him about two feet away and just stared into his eyes. Mike felt they were waiting either for a reaction from him or orders from within the craft. After what seemed like an age they moved forward and took up position around him, two in front two behind, facing the craft. Mike could feel the sensation of thoughts being beamed towards him. He tried to blank them out and keep his mind focused. This came easy to him due to his anti-interrogation training, but he could feel the invasion of his mind becoming stronger. At this point Mike decided to walk forwards to the craft and see the reaction, this seemed to work as the sensations stopped and the four aliens joined him and walked up the vamp.

They entered the craft into a corridor which was white and shiny with a continuous carved ceiling which merged into the walls and floor, with no visible joins. The corridor curved around and appeared to be following the perimeter of the craft. There were concealed lights at high and low levels and every six to eight feet there were portholes looking to the outside. At the end of the corridor was a dead-end wall, but as they approached the wall opened as a door. They walked through and it closed behind them. Further on they went through another door and entered a room with two fitted built-in type seats. One of the aliens pointed for Mike to sit down. This was the first sign of communication. Mike sat down and three of the aliens left the room leaving one to stand guard. As Mike looked at his watch he noticed that it had stopped, so he could not tell how long this would last.

Some time passed and the door opened and he was ushered through what seemed like a medical room. This was a large white room with a fixed table in the centre, and there was unequal equipment under the table and fixed to the walls and ceiling. Above the table was a large scanner-type machine, there were lights all around the room – it was very bright and light.

Mike was taken to the table and he sat on one end, and then a team of five aliens entered the room. They must have been the medical team; they had similar features but had different uniforms, silver in colour and fitting. The original guard stood in the corner next to the door. The leader of the team pointed to Mike to lie down. At this point Mike could feel anxiety creeping in, he had to really focus his mind to overcome this. They lowered the scanning machine over him close to his chest and from under the table they released equipment that looked like probes and attached them to his legs and arms. Then one of the team pulled a lever and the scanner lit up. As the lights increased the arm and legs lit up and changed colour.

All of a sudden there was a bang and the team moved back. When Mike looked down he could see the fingers on his false arm had fixed together. One of the team left the room and returned with another alien. This one was different from the others, taller, and his uniform was very elaborate. It was blue in colour and brightly decorated with symbols on the chest. The belt and neck collar were studded with diamond shaped crystals and the boots had the same features on the sides. He looked at Mike, who was still lying down, and the medical leader pointed to Mike's arm. Mike thought he should react so he took his arm off and showed his stump. The new alien who Mike thought must be their leader picked it up and inspected the arm, at the same time he seemed to be discussing it with the medical team using telepathy.

After a while the leader came over to Mike and touched him in the shoulder and stared into his eyes. Mike could feel the sensation that he had earlier, he thought the leader was trying to communicate using telepathy and Mike decided to let it happen. He just opened his mind and the alien introduced himself as the leader in command of the craft, and his name was Sharaze. He asked Mike who he was and what he was doing in this place alone and what was the story of his arm. Mike struggled to respond at first but he soon found it quite easy. He just thought rather than spoke the words.

Mike explained how he had lost his arm while fighting the terrorists who are enemies of the free people and who threatened World peace. He told Sharaze he had come to this place alone to consider how he could continue his fight now he had only one hand. Sharaze asked Mike if he would allow him to carry out some more tests so that he could understand more of what happened and Mike agreed. He lay down and the medical team attached a helmet and probes to Mike and fixed the other end to a machine. To the side of the machine was a screen a bit like a television. Sharaze told Mike to go through in his mind events of the past leading up to his accident with his arm.

Mike was astounded that his thoughts were being relayed to the screen and as he went through the events he watched the screen show in detail every thought. It was like watching a film and at the end Sharaze came over to him again, putting his hand on his shoulder. Sharaze said they were doing similar jobs and that he too was involved in protecting his world, watching other worlds to see if they posed any threat. He had visited Earth many times over the years and it was a concern of his leaders the way war raged all over his world and that one day it would destroy itself.

Sharaze told Mike of his world where there was no fighting and how life was so peaceful but needed to be protected. He said his world was in a parallel universe to ours and that their concern was that if our world was destroyed it would destabilise our universe and in turn affect theirs.

Sharaze told Mike he would be taken to a rest room and could bathe, eat and sleep and they would talk again the following day. As he left the room Sharaze again touched Mike on the shoulder. One of the guards took him back along the corridor into a small room. There was a table set with same fruit and a jug with some red liquid inside. There were a further two rooms. One with a bed and a robe laid on the top and in the other room there was washing facilities. After bathing and eating he drank the liquid then put on the rope and climbed into bed. He was tired after such an ordeal but found it difficult to sleep. Mike was very taken with Sharaze, he felt he could trust him, he thought he was a good and honourable being.

Next morning he was awakened by the guard who then left the room. Mike washed and dressed then sat on the bed wondering what the day had in store. He felt quite excited, he had slept in a UFO and talked to the leader. What was to follow, he wondered. Just then the door opened and Sharaze entered. He asked Mike if he had slept and if he was feeling refreshed. Mike thanked him and asked what was going to happen next. Sharaze asked Mike if he would like to see his world and see how beautiful and peaceful it was. Mike would be honoured and was very excited at the prospect.

He followed Sharaze back through the corridors to the medical room. He sat on the bed and one of the medical team came into the room with a long box. Inside was an arm very similar to the one that had fused. As they fitted the arm Mike could not feel it because it was so comfortable. It was much better than his original. It felt almost as good as his real arm, he could bend the elbow and the hand was incredible, all the joints moved with strength and feeling. Around the wrist was a band with four crystals, the same crystals that Sharaze had on his belt and neck collar. Sharaze told him it would take time to get used to his new arm it was very high tech and the strength in the hand was many times stronger than his real hand.

Sharaze told Mike to follow him as he walked out of the room, they went along a different corridor and ended up in what looked like the engine room or control room of the craft. There was fixed bench furniture with built-in control panels. Under what looked like the main control panel there were a number of different sized and coloured crystals. They were oscillating and giving off a low-key humming sound. There were fixed seats in front of these panels with what appeared to be restraining belts.

Then Sharaze showed Mike his hand with crystals the same as the one Mike had on the wrist of his new hand. He told Mike to turn the hand anti-clockwise and to Mikes amazement they both disappeared. They were still in the craft but invisible and he could see everything in the room. Sharaze explained they had moved into the fourth dimension. He went on to say that they called this the observation zone, they could see things that were happening without being detected. They used this zone to keep a check on things that were happening in other worlds, and had done this for centuries. Sharaze told Mike to concentrate his thoughts to go forward. Sharaze went first, he just floated forward and Mike followed. They went straight through the sides of the craft and floated on up to the trees and continued straight through the trees. Again Sharaze explained that with them being in a different dimension then any sold matter was in the other dimension and so they could float through.

Sharaze then told Mike to turn his band anti-clockwise

again and as they did the crystals lit up and started to oscillate then the trees and surroundings disappeared and they were standing in a different place. Sharaze explained this was his world. The observation zone was like a vacuum between their two worlds, parallel universes separated by a fourth dimension.

The countryside was beautiful, so green and lush with strange plants and trees, the sky had a red glow so clear in the distance he could see mountains and a large river running down one side. Further on there was a large city. There were walkways at a high level with beings moving in all directions. These walkways linked all parts of the city. There was no sign of transport. Sharaze explained all transport was underground – a network shuttle serviced the whole city in fast comfortable vehicles. Other parts of the country and the rest of their world was serviced by shuttle space craft which left from each city.

Their lives were very calm and peaceful with no wars and very little disturbance. As they headed back Sharaze explained how his world had troubles in the past and wars and they too had fought to save their world. This only came about when all world leaders came together and crushed the trouble makers. 'Now there is no starvation or poverty. Our nations are content with their lives and their environment.'

They turned their bands clockwise once into the

observation zone and clockwise again and they were back inside the craft. Sharaze explained when the band is turned the crystals generated a shaft of light which transports them anti-clockwise to go and clockwise to return. Sharaze told Mike he must keep the band and use it to fight the terrorists that threatened their worlds. He must keep this his secret. No one must be told about their meeting or the band. He said that if at any time there was a situation that Mike could not solve himself and it threatened the security or safety of their worlds if he turned the band twice Sharaze would come to his aid.

As they said their goodbyes and Mike left the craft Sharaze knew Mike was a special man, someone he could trust, dedicated to bringing peace to his world. He was sure this would not be the last time they would meet as he watched Mike disappear behind the trees. That night Mike could not sleep as he lay in his tent. He went over everything that had happened and he wondered how he could use the band without others finding out. Next day he must try out the band to make sure it really did work and that he had not dreamt it. He was up early and he turned the band and sure enough he become invisible. He floated through the forest passing through the trees. There was a deer up ahead so he floated up to it and stopped up close, the deer did not move it could not see nor smell him.

For the rest of the day he continued to think of the best use of his newfound weapon, and the words of Sharaze had said about all of his world leaders working together to defeat evil. Mike came up with the idea of forming an international 'Ghost Force' to wage war on terror. Most countries have their own special force, each one would provide one of their best men who would meet and train together at Hereford and return to their own force until they were needed. A team from these men would be selected depending on the mission and special requirements. Depending on the location of the mission and what sort of expertise was required the troops would be selected and briefed at Hereford. The size of the team would again depend on the mission and how many specialist troopers were needed such as demolitionists, snipers, weapons, signals and communications, first aid, jungle warfare and close quarter combat to name a few.

Mike would carry out the reconnaissance using his band to gather the intelligence required to pass on to the team led by Steve from Delta Force. Steve had over the years proved to be the best man in Delta Force. He had led many missions and was a specialist with weapons. He was admired by all his fellow troopers and looked upon as being invincible, a real James Bond.

Now Mike must go back to Hereford and convince Commander James Brown, without revealing his invisible secret weapon. Back at HQ Mike put his idea to James, but the commander had doubts about Mikes mental and physical strength after his ordeal with his arm. Mike suggests that he be set a task to prove he still had what it takes to make his idea work. James told him the biggest test would be to return to Iraq and gather intelligence of Saddam's supporters, hideouts and arms dumps.

Mike went back to Iraq and made such a success of the mission that James agreed to discuss the idea with the home office. A meeting was then arranged in America between commanding officers from Delta Force and the SAS. Mike and Steve were there but were told to wait outside while the meeting took place. On the second day of the meetings Mike and Steve were called in to be told that two high-profile hostages had been taken in Afghanistan, one American one British. It had been decided that Mike should go there at once and see if he could find out clues as to their whereabouts. Meanwhile as assault team of troopers would be assembled and sent over to act on Mike's information.

The two diplomats were inspecting a hospital just outside Kabul with security guards following behind them. After the inspection they left the hospital to go to their car. Two ambulances that were parked nearby started up and slowly headed towards them. The first ambulance headed for the guards and started shooting, the second one pulled up beside the diplomats and bundled them inside. The two ambulances sped over to the gates the one with the diplomats drove through the other ambulance stopped in front of the gates blocking it off. The rebels jumped out and climbed into the other ambulance and as they sped off the one blocking the gates and blew up.

A helicopter was called in to follow the ambulance but as it reached the foot of a range of mountains it turned onto a side road and stopped. The helicopter hovered overhead but then the ambulance began to sink and disappear underground. On landing, the helicopter crew found the area where the ambulance had been. They searched and found a void in the ground, below was rail track inside a large tunnel. The ambulance must have been lowered on some sort of hydraulic lift onto the rail track. All of a sudden there was a huge explosion and smoke was gashing from the hole. The rebels must have blown up the tunnel preventing being followed.

The American and British Embassies informed the military office and they contacted the two special forces. So Mike went to the area where the ambulance disappeared. He climbed down the hole and followed the rail track to where the tunnel had been blocked. He turned his band and became invisible. He floated through the rubble of the explosion and continued following the track for about a mile. The track branched three ways, as he inspected the tracks he could see the dirt had been removed from one of them. He followed that track for a further mile and came to a guard with a machine gun. Further on there was a wide open area and the ambulance was parked at one side on a flat rail truck, it was empty and further on there was a group of rebels. As he got closer he could see the two diplomats tied up and being questioned by two of the rebels.

After half an hour the prisoners were taken through one of the tunnels and Mike followed. After a short walk they opened a door into a room. It was small and dark with only a small light, there was straw on the floor and the prisoners were made to lie on it. They were tied together as they lay down and the guards left the room, locked the door and made their way back to the main area.

Mike went back into the tunnel and followed the track away from the main area for about two miles were there was a dead end. It was a solid stone wall built to seal the tunnel, Mike floated through and then followed the track. A mile further on there was another cave in and when Mike floated through the rubble he was outside. This was the back entrance to the mine but was blocked with the rubble from an explosion. He made his way back to the main area and counted some hundred men. They had mortars and machine guns at the front entrance to the cave and ten guards. This entrance was difficult to find as it was covered with bushes and vegetation and set in the mountain rocks. Mike got his bearings so that he would be able to plot the details on a map back at base and headed back the way he came in.

Back at HQ he was called to a meeting with the special forces commanders in chief and Steve was there as he would lead the assault team. Mike described the situation and plotted the details onto a map of the area showing the position of the rebels tunnels and the front and rear entrances. The agreed plan was that Steve would take a team of five troopers including himself, two specialising in demolition, one in signals, one medical and Steve in weapons. They would go to the rear entrance and using explosives they would clear the entrance. To cover the explosion at the same time the American commander would mortar the front entrance. Then Steve's team would enter the tunnel and again using explosives would demolish the stone wall leaving a clear run to the prisoners.

The only problem would be if the rebels realised that the rear entrance and the wall had been cleared they could then get to the prisoners first, Mike said that if he was briefed by the demolition trooper then he could set the explosives at the entrance from the main area to the tunnel where the prisoners were being held. This would seal off the prisoners from the rebels but it would mean Steve would have to get to them, otherwise they would be in a sealed tomb. This would also trap the rebels with no exit and enable the Commandos to finish the job. The SAS commander wanted Mike to take the demolition trooper with him but Mike said that he had more chance of success on his own. He said once they heard the internal explosion then that would be the signal for the attack to start at both entrances. Once the prisoners were freed they would make their way back to the rear entrance and would contact base and a helicopter would pick them up. The attack was planned just before dawn as most of the rebels would still be sleeping and Mike would be able to set the explosives without being detected.

On the day Mike was invisible as he checked the prisoners to make sure there were no guards in their room and none in the outside tunnel. Back in the main area the rebels were all asleep, the guards were still at the front entrance but well away from where Mike was to set the explosives. Standing in the tunnel be detonated the explosives bringing the roof down at the entrance and sealing the tunnel. He then turned his band again and waited inside the room with the prisoners just in case he was needed. The operation went smoothly. It was great success with no causalities in the American or British camps.

Back at HQ going through the mission and how events had unfolded questions were asked by the Commandos about how Mike was able to get in and out without being detected. Mike said that's what made him good at his job and that he must keep his techniques a secret so that he could use them in future. James Brown said the only answer he had come up with was that Mike was invisible, they all laughed.

So it was the success of this mission that proved Mike's idea of an International Ghost Force was sound, and had the backing of most of the special forces commanders. Over the next few weeks troopers from special forces all over the world one from each country arrived at Hereford. They trained together and Mike and Steve vetted the individual troopers noting their specialised area to use in future missions. They all returned to their regiments and would be called when needed depending on the mission at hand.

There was continued trouble in Iraq and again the commanders of the special forces were called to a meeting. An American military base twenty miles south of Bagdad had been taken by Fedaveen troops loyal to Saddam Hussein and approximately five hundred troops were being held prisoners. The Fedaveen had attacked in force a small garrison some ten miles away from the military base knowing they would send troops to aid the garrison. This would leave the base vulnerable to attack and while the fighting was taking place at the garrison some two thousand Fedaveen soldiers attacked the base and overpowered the remaining American troops. Two tracks packed with explosives rammed the checkpoint at the main gates, destroying the guard house and killing the troops inside. The rebels flooded through, shooting at any resistance. Most of the troops were in the mess or their barracks and were soon overpowered.

The Americans were rounded up and put in a large aeroplane hanger and tied up, their officers were taken to be interrogated. The officers were told to contact their HQ and relay the rebels demands, which were that the five hundred prisoners would be exchanged for the Iraqi prisoners, including a list of important prisoners the Americans were holding. They would have one week to agree and then ten American prisoners would be shot every day.

When the news reached the American's HQ there was an emergency meeting called with the coalition officers and the special forces. James Brown suggested sending in his reconnaissance man that night and they would meet again next day. This was agreed and James sent for Mike, who had just arrived in Iraq after working in Afghanistan. As soon as he was briefed he set off for the base. He left his jeep some quarter of a Mike from the base. It was dark and he was able to get near to the base before turning his hand and becoming invisible. As he floated through the damaged front check point which had been repaired, there were two guards at the side. Each corner of the base housed a guard with a machine gun, elevated on towers facing out from the base watching for any activity. The mess room and barracks were filled with Iraqi troops. The building that contained all the arms was stocked with rifles, machine guns, mortars, and an assortment of weapons left by the Americans. The building was alarmed and very secure. Further on was the hanger where the prisoners were being held. Mike entered and saw the prisoners lying on straw on the floor with their hands tied behind them, and there was a guard sitting with a rifle near the door.

Outside the hanger there was another two guards sitting on chairs talking, their rifles were propped up against the wall. Mike stayed to watch the events of the night, things that might help in the planned attack. At twelve o'clock nine men came out of the barracks and each one made his way to a guard position. The guards that had been on duty made their way back to the barracks and Mike waited a while and saw there was no more activity. He continued around the base doing a full check on the other buildings. He came across the power station which housed all the electrics for the base. He decided to knock out the main switch and see what reaction there was from the guards. So he turned his band and turned the main switch off. Turning his band again he floated outside to see the response from the guards. It was pitch black and the guards shouted at each other. One of the guards outside the hanger went to the mess room and returned with a torch. He went behind the power station to a small hut, Mike followed him to see what he was doing. There was a generator inside and after few minutes it started up and the base was lit with a few temporary lights until six o'clock when the guards changed again. Mike put the switch back on and left to return to his HQ and report his findings.

Later on he met up with James and the other commanders and he went through the information he had collected. The Americans had a detailed layout of the base and Mike marked up the positions of the guards and the prisoners and the fire power. Mike's plan would see him turning the power off and throwing a rope ladder over the wall behind the arms building. This was out of sight of all the guards. Steve would lead a ten-man team from International Ghost Force over the wall once the power was switched off. They would take out the guard that came to switch the generator on and then while the base was in darkness take out the guards and replace them.

They would then put the generator on and with the machine guns turned to face the barracks and mess room Steve and the other troopers would release the prisoners. Mike would have disarmed the alarm on the arms building when he turned off the power so Steve could arm all the prisoners once released. They would wait till the first light and the coalition troops would enter the base and join the released prisoners to take up their positions. Then in force they would enter the barracks and mess room to take the rebels by surprise.

This plan was agreed but Mike said he would return to the base that night and make sure there were no changes in the routine of the rebels and if he turned the power off again they would not suspect anything on the night of the attack. Mike went through the same procedure watching the guards change then he waited awhile before switching off the power. The same guard from beside the hanger came and turned on the generator before turning to his post. Mike waited till morning, put the power back on before returning HQ.

Another meeting took place with the commanders of the special forces, Steve and Mike discussed the details of the mission. The critical area was the guards, who must be overpowered without raising the alarm.

Steve selected his ten-man team who were all experts in martial arts and hand-to-hand combat. They were flown in the next day from the special forces from all over the world and are brought into the mission.

The mission goes to plan; Mike waits until the guard have changed shifts and settled down, he waits till two o'clock and turns the power off and the alarm to the arms building. He throws the rope ladder over the wall and turns invisible to watch the guards as Steve and his team climb the wall. The rest of the plan goes like clockwork. They take out the guards without a sound and take over the machine guns. Steve and three troopers replace the prisoners and arm them under cover of their fellow troopers on the machine guns. At five thirty the armed prisoners cover the barracks and mess room as the coalition troops creep into the base. Once all are in position they raid the buildings and take over the base without casualty.

Back at HQ the commanders and the troopers of the special forces go through the mission and all agreed this was a near perfect mission. The powers that be had little doubt that the International Ghost Force was indeed an important tool in the future of their war on terror. Mike and Steve were proving to be an awesome combination and were gaining respect from their commanders and fellow troopers.

Mike and Steve had just returned from two weeks leave at Steve's home in America, spending time with Steve's girlfriend and his sister Holly. They had been back at their Iraq headquarters when they were asked to attend a meeting with their special forces commanders. One of the main roads into the Afghanistan city of Kabul used by the coalition troops to transport supplies and equipment had been taken by the Taliban. The road passed by the foot of a mountain range and they had dug into the side of the mountain, destroying passing coalition transport. They had everything in place including a large contingent of troops at the base of the mountain and were well armed. They were protected from a higher level with mortars and at a higher level again by surface-to-air missiles. These missiles had destroyed two helicopters and one aeroplane the Americans had sent in to flush out the enemy.

The other side of the mountain was a sheer cliff and could not be climbed by American commandos who had been sent to investigate. So the commanders of the special forces had been asked to look at the situation and see what they could come up with. It was decided that Mike would go and carry out his reconnaissance and report back with details as soon as possible. Next day Mike flew to Afghanistan and was taken to the American base camp some three miles from the enemy's position. They took him by jeep to a position just out of sight of the enemy and he was told they would return to the same spot in four hours. Mike watched the jeep disappear towards base. He turned his hand and became invisible. He floated towards the foot of the mountain. There were bunkers all around the base full of troops, equipment, rifles with grenade launchers, machine guns and stocks of ammunition. At a higher there were three bunkers with mortar tubes and large stocks of mortars in each, attended by two rebels in each bunker. At the highest level some five hundred yards from the top of the mountain were three surface-to-air missile launchers again with a stock of stinger missiles.

There was a dirt track road winding up from the base of the mountain to the missile position. When Mike reached the top and looked down he could see that they were covering the whole side of the mountain. There were no guards on the back face of the mountain as it was a sheer cliff face. Mike went down that side and found there were caves set into the mountain face at different levels. He thought it may be possible to scale that side, climbing from cave to cave at the different levels. On the way back down he made a mental note of the position of the bunkers at each level and the numbers of rebels in each.

As he left the mountain and returned to his pick-up point he thought of a plan to put to his commanders.

When he reached the American base he was surprised to see James Brown and Steve had flown in to be at the meeting. Mike marked up the plan provided by the Americans plotting the positions of the rebel troops and their firepower. They discussed different ideas, Mike's idea was that Steve should lead the Ghost Force to the rear of the mountain. They would climb to the top using ropes that Mike had put in place from one level to another linking the caves to reach the top. Mike and Steve agreed the team would be made up of two troopers specialised in mountaineering, one Italian, one from New Zealand, one martial arts expert from Japan, one demolition expert from Australia, one communications expert from Britain (SAS) and Steve specialised in weapons. The following day these troopers were flown from duty with their special forces to join the briefing of the International Ghost Force.

At the meeting the mountaineers explained to Mike what they would need and how he would secure the rope lines at each level. Then Mike said once they reached to top using their night vision goggles they must make their way over to the front edge of the mountain. He would leave three marks on the top showing the positions of the missile launchers directly below. The team would split into three pairs to tackle the three launchers, then abseil down to the side of the bunkers. Then on a prearranged signal they would rush the three positions, at the same time taking out the rebels. Once secured they would make their way down the track and take out the mortar positions again using their night vision goggles.

The Australian demolition trooper would set explosives on the track further down the mountain covered by Steve with his machine gun. This would prevent their troops escaping up the mountain once the attack started. When all this was in position they would contact base and order the air attack to start. At the first air strike they would detonate the explosives and blow the track, and then fire mortars down onto the bunkers at the base of the mountain. They would then retreat to the top of the mountain while the air raids bombarded the enemy positions. The artillery and tank divisions would add to the attack and finally the Commandos would move in using hand grenades to clear the bunkers.

The plan was agreed but questioned how Mike would put the first part of the plan into operation. How would he be able to put the ropes in place? Mike explained that by himself he would be able to move up the mountain with the equipment without being detected as he had done the day before. He would contact base once the ropes were in position, and if they did not hear from him they should abort the mission.

The following day just before dusk Mike was

dropped off at the other side of the mountain with the equipment the two mountaineers had supplied. It was very lightweight. When the jeep left him he sorted the equipment into four sections and putting the first set of tackle and rope on his shoulder turned invisible. He floated to the first level and found a place in a cave to secure the first rope. Once secured he dropped the rope down to the ground. At each level he turned invisible to carry the equipment to the next level, turned his band again to float back down to the ground to pick up the next set of equipment.

Once they were all in position he floated back down, making sure they were all in place. He then returned to the top to make the three marks for the position of their launchers using his band again he was able to float up directly above each position and mark it with luminous paint spray. He then contacted base to confirm success. While he waited for the team to arrive he checked each level to make sure the rebels had not heard him with the ropes being secured. He was pleased to see that the rebels were still in their places and Steve and his team would find everything as discussed at the briefing. He then went back to the other side to wait for the team. If only they knew he was watching over them they would have felt a lot happier.

As Steve and his team started to climb the mountain

they had a little light from the moon and when they reached the first level they felt more confident. After two hours they reached the top and as they crept over the front edge they were pleased to see the luminous marks. They abseiled down in pairs landing about two hundred yards from each missile position, and when Steve gave the signal they went in together to secure the three positions. They met up and using their night vision goggles they made their way down the track to the next level, and one by one they took over the mortar positions. Then Steve and the demolition expert went further down the track. He set the explosives while Steve kept watch, then they made their way back up and joined the rest of the team. The communications troopers contacted Base to say everything was ready while the other troopers loaded the mortars.

Some half an hour later the first sound of the air attack could be heard as the helicopter gunships came from behind the mountain. As they opened fire Steve gave the signal to blow up the track and release the mortars at will. Over the following hour the foot of the mountain was bombarded with mortars and wave after wave of air attacks. Steve and his team made their way to the top of the mountain as the artillery and tank divisions moved into continue the bombardment. After some time they stopped and Steve and his team watched as the Commandos moved in and cleaned out the bombers out as they worked down the line. The mission was a great success with no coalition causalities and another feather in the cap of the International Ghost Force.

American intelligence informed that AL Qaeda had linked up with terrorist groups in several countries and had been working together on a nuclear programme. Since the break up of Russia, some of their nuclear weapons and technology had been sold to various terrorist networks. Their pooled resources had enabled them to develop rockets with nuclear warheads, and had them sited in different parts of the world in secret locations.

They had made certain demands and if these were not met then the rockets would be launched at the same time causing havoc all over the world. Their demands were:

1. All their prisoners be released from American, Arabic, Western, Persian, Jewish jails.
2. That the war against Islam and Muslims around the world be stopped.
3. That land be returned to them, including Jerusalem and Kashmir.
4. America stop interfering in Muslim countries and that they be allowed to set up an Islamic state.

There was an urgent meeting with the American president the British prime minister and their defence leaders. This had to be top secret and must be dealt with by the special forces. There was a further meeting involving the commanders of the British and American special forces and they were briefed on the dangerous situation. They were told that this was top secret as AL Qaeda had warned that if one site was attacked then all the rockets would be launched without further warning.

So it was agreed that the International Ghost Force would be asked to carry out reconnaissance and report back once the sites had been located. James Brown sent for Mike and he was briefed on the facts and information that they had and the importance of the mission. James suggested that Mike take a team with him in order to locate all the sites, but Mike said he worked better on his own. He said that he would be less conspicuous by himself and would be able to move in places that a team would be seen and put the mission at risk. He asked for forty-eight hours, and if he had no success then James could send in a team. James agreed but insisted on an update in that time.

Mike knew what he must do, it would be impossible for him to locate all the sites on his own in forty-eight hours. There was only one way he could do this and that was to ask for help from his alien friend Sharaze. This was exactly the situation that Sharaze had told Mike if he found himself in that he should contact him. If those rockets were launched they would destroy parts of the world and the repercussions could lead to a full world nuclear war.

So Mike made his way to Exmoor and found the place where he first met Sharaze. He stood on the spot where the space craft had landed and he turned his band twice. He was transported to the world of Sharaze. He stood for a while and realised this was the place he had visited before, so he started to make his way towards the city. A bright light flashed over his head and as he turned he could see a space craft landing when the ramp came down Mike was to see Sharaze walk down. They greeted each other like long lost brothers. Sharaze invited Mike to join him on the craft. They communicated for a while catching up with events since their last meeting. Then Mike told him of the problem and said it would be impossible for him to solve this on his own and asked for Sharaze's help. Sharaze agreed and said the first job was to locate on the sites. He asked Mike if he had any idea of the location of any of them. Mike told him that the terrorists had made threats against Britain, Italy, Australia, Japan and America. Mike suggested that Italy might be the best place to start. Sharaze told him that they would need to travel together to gather the information needed.

Sharaze showed Mike a map of the world on one of the screens and asked him to touch the screen showing Italy. A detailed map of Italy came up on the screen and Sharaze gave the crew orders to take off. Mike could not believe that he was in an alien space craft travelling through space on a mission. They travelled in the observation zone so they would not be detected, and after a short trip they landed. Sharaze explained they had landed in Italy and would wait until nightfall before changing to our dimension, they started to fly across the country scanning the land Sharaze explained if there were nuclear weapons present they be picked up by the computer from the scanner.

As night fell the craft moved from the observation Zone into our dimension and following a grid system on the screen made a search of the land working from north to south. Working across the country until they flew over the Dolomites in the north east of the country. Some thirty-five miles from Venice the computer indicated a nuclear reading. They moved back into the observation zone and landed at the foot of the Dolomites in a clearing along the valley floor.

Sharaze and Mike floated through the woods and entered towers of limestone crags that formed the base of the Dolomites. They came across a camp which was sheltered by the walls of the mountain and hidden with vegetation and trees at the front making it difficult to find. The camp was well set up with sleeping quarters and a mess room and a large cave stocked with an assortment of weapons and firepower. There was somewhere near a thousand rebels made up of mostly terrorists from the Red Brigade. Further on they saw the rocket standing at the entrance of a cave complete with warhead and launcher. Again it was camouflaged with vegetation and trees. There was a power room which was made up of banks of generators, and leading from this was a control room with computer screens and communication system. There were ten workers all dressed in white uniforms seated beside the screens using the communication system.

Sharaze floated over to the computer screens and watched intently for some time, then he signalled to Mike to leave. They floated back through the caves and back to their space craft and control room. He set up one of the computers and typed in some figures and the computer lit up. Again he typed in some information to the computer and a detailed map of Venezuela in South America appeared on the screen. Then a close up of the Flat Top Mountains and Angel Falls came up on the screen. Sharaze explained to Mike that they were the co-ordinates from the rebels computers indicating their central control headquarters.

So they set off for South America again using the observation zone, and touching down at the foot of Flat Top Mountain. Again Mike and Sharaze left the craft in the area of Autana which had caves carved into the sheer sides of the mountains. They came across a large camp similar to the one in Italy with all the facilities to sustain a large army. Further into the mountains there was a power room and control centre more elaborate than the Italian centre, with banks of computers and satellite communications. There were thirty white uniformed workers and outside the room four guards were on standby.

In the outside camp there were fifteen hundred rebels made up from different nationalities and armed with heavy firepower including missile launchers, machine guns and a huge assortment of weapons. The rocket was sited in a cave entrance next to the control room, camouflaged and guarded by ten rebels. Again Sharaze went over to the computers and watched for some time, then signalled for Mike to leave. They returned to their craft and back to the control room, where Sharaze set up the computer and feeds in the information he had gleaned from the rebels' computers. The computer printed out details of all the rocket sites and the co-ordinates needed to be able to visit each location. Mike had completed a report of the two sites they had been to with the numbers of troops and weapons, the layout of the camps and control rooms and position of the rocket sites.

Sharaze said they would visit the remaining sites so that would complete his reconnaissance and report each set when he returned to his HQ. The other sites were located in Japan, Mount Fuji some sixty miles southwest of Tokyo, Australia, the Eucalyptus forest of the Warrambungle mountains some one hundred and eighty miles from Sydney, Turkey, Cappadocia's Cones, Central Turkey, Ireland, the cliffs of Moheron the west coast.

They set off and visited each site using the observation zone and then left the craft. While Mike carried out his reconnaissance Sharaze gleamed details from the computers. All the sites were very similar in the way they were set up and defended, and at the end of the day Mike had a pull report on each one. They flew back to the world of Sharaze and Mike spent the night there. Next morning feeling refreshed they discussed their findings and plans. Sharaze pointed out that the problems for Mike and his forces were being able to take all of the sites at the same time without the rockets either being launched or blown up. This is where he could help. He could send a space craft to each site and immobilise the mechanical and electrical power in each area.

Each craft would send a beam of power covering the whole area of the rebels' camp and rocket site. This would prevent the rebels launching the rockets or using their computer or communications equipment. The beam would also join all weapons in the area so this would prevent the rebels using their weapons on Mike's troops or blowing up the rockets. This of course would apply to Mike's troop – they would not be able to use their weapons and would have to rely on physical strength to overpower the rebels. Mike replied this would not be a problem as his troops would be hand-picked experts in hand-to-hand combat. Sharaze explained that his presence must be kept secret and that with the site's co-ordinates they would be able to emit the rays from the observation zone. Mike must go back to HQ and brief. James Brown and plan the operation on each site and then come back to Sharaze to confirm times and dates of the attacks. They said their goodbyes and Mike returned to his world and made his way back to HQ.

He went directly to James and showed him his reports and plans of the attacks. James was astounded by the information and wondered how Mike could have been to all the sites in such a short time. Mike went on to say that all the sites must be attacked at the same time and that no weapons would be used. The use of any firepower could blow up the rockets and kill their whole force. Each site must be attacked by a team made up of special forces and Commandos all trained in hand-to-and combat. The leader of the team would be the trooper from that country's special force who had trained with the International Ghost Force.

So in Venezuela Steve would lead Delta Force and the American Commandos, and with each team would be a weapons inspector specialising in nuclear weapons able to disarm the rocket warheads. Also a communication expert would be with each team to keep contact with the other sites and make sure they attacked at the same time. James had one question – if our troops are not armed how will the rebels be disarmed, and who would stop them using their weapons? Mike asked James to trust him as he had in past missions and all would go well with this mission. James agrees to go along with Mike's plan but told him if things went wrong it would be the end of the International Ghost Force and both their careers.

The following day the commanders of the special forces and commanders from the countries involved were told to fly to Hereford for a briefing. James had his work cut out to convince them that they must not take weapons on this mission but they compromised by agreeing to carry hand guns. This would make the troops feel safer and the guns would be used only in an emergency if the rebels had weapons. A base camp would be set up some one mile from each site, with back-up troops and heavy firepower and they would move in if things went wrong. Once the attacks had commenced the communications trooper would signal to the base camps and they would send troops to capture the escaping rebels. The plan was agreed and the attacks were planned for one week's time, confirmation would be given two days before.

The next morning Mike contacted Sharaze and went through the plan. He asked if he would be able to have his spacecrafts in place in the time given. Sharaze confirmed there would be no problems and that he would have them in place the night before. He assured Mike that all the weapons would be out of action and took out a strange looking gun which emitted the same ray as the beam of the spacecrafts. He pointed the ray at Mike and asked him to try and fire his handgun. Mike pulled the trigger and was relieved when it jammed. Sharaze told Mike to join him the day before the attack and they would watch over the operation from the space craft.

James and Mike flew to each country and visited each HQ inspecting their troops and checking that the operation and training was going to plan. Two days before the attack everything was in place and all the troops were ready to move into position.

The attack was planned for the Monday and Mike joined Sharaze on the Sunday morning and after going over the operation one last time they set off for Venezuela. Sharaze explained they would monitor this site as it was the central control HQ and they would be on hand if things did go wrong. When they reached the site they landed in the observation zone and prepared for the following day. Sharaze set the co-ordinates for the six sites into the computers and the sites appeared on each of the six screens. They would be able to watch each operation as it unfolded and check that everything was going to plan.

On the Monday morning Sharaze and Mike watched as the rays were beamed down onto each site and soon after they saw the troops move into each location and advance on the rebel camps. The commanders led the advance and tackled the main body of rebel troops. Mike was relieved to see the rebels' weapons were unable to fire. Then the special forces entered the caves wearing their night vision goggles as the power had been immobilised and everywhere was in darkness. The main body of rebels were outnumbered on each site and were soon overpowered. Some escaped but the troops from the base camp were there to mop up. Mike and Sharaze had to wait some time before they could see the white-coated rebels being led out of the caves guarded by the special forces and after what seemed like a lifetime for Mike, Steve was the first out with hands in the air in triumph.

Mike thanked Sharaze and again he was told to contact Sharaze any time he needed his help and he was sure they would meet again. Mike left and returned to his HQ and James was delighted with one hundred per cent success, no casualties and most of the rebels taken prisoner. He looked at Mike and smiled. He said he did not know how Mike had completed this mission but knew he must have had help. He went on to say this would be Mike's secret and as long as the missions were a success the future of the International Ghost Force was assured. James said Mike deserved some leave after a long and draining mission. So he again joined Steve and they returned to America to see Steve's girlfriend and Holly.

What did the future hold for Mike and Steve in their war on terror? With the help of the International Ghost Force they could tackle missions all over the world, Sharaze would play a big role in ensuring the safety of our world and assist Mike when called upon. Mike got closer to Holly on his many visits to America.